Crafty Coaching!

Michael Coleman
Illustrated by Nick Abadzis

ORCHARD BOOKS

ORCHARD BOOKS
96 Leonard Street, London EC2A 4XD
Orchard Books Australia
Unit 31/56 O'Riordan Street, Alexandria NSW 2015
First published in Great Britain in 2000
First paperback edition 2001
Text © Michael Coleman, 2000
Illustrations © Nick Abadzis, 2000
Cover photograph © Professional Sport
The rights of Michael Coleman to be identified as the author
and Nick Abadzis as the illustrator of this work
have been asserted by them in accordance with the
Copyright, Designs and Patents Act, 1988.
A CIP catalogue record for this book is available
from the British Library.
ISBN 1 84121 509 0 (hbk)
ISBN 1 84121 511 2 (pbk)
1 3 5 7 9 10 8 6 4 2 (hbk)
1 3 5 7 9 10 8 6 4 2 (pbk)
Printed in Great Britain

Contents

Coach

Left Full
Back

Midfield
(Centre)

Striker

Right Full
Back

Centre
Back

Goalkeeper

Kirsten
Browne

Barry 'Bazza'
Watts

Tarlock
Bhasin

Lennie
Gould
(captain)

Daisy
Higgins

Colin 'Colly'
Flower

Trev the
Rev

Substitute

Midfield
(Centre)

Centre
Back

Midfield
(Right)

Striker

Substitute

Midfield
(Left)

Mick
Ryall

Jonjo
Rix

Lulu
Squibb

Jeremy
Emery

Rhoda
O'Neill

Lionel
Murgatroyd

Ricky
King

1

The Angels Code

Peeeeeeeeeeeeeeeeeeeeeeeeeeeeeeeeeeeeeeeeeppp!!!!!

As the piercing sound cut across their training pitch, the whole Angels squad forgot about football and dived for cover with their hands over their ears.

"Wh-what was that?" mumbled Jeremy Emery, when the sound had finally faded away. "A rocket?"

"A jet fighter. Nothing less," said Tarlock Bhasin.

It was Kirsten Browne who was brave enough to put her head out from beneath her goalkeeper's jersey and see the real cause. "It was Trev! Look! He's over there."

The Angels coach was sitting in his car, a small suitcase on the seat beside him. "Sorry to frighten you, gang. I've been practising my whistling."

"That was a whistle?" said Lionel Murgatroyd. "It sounded more like a train entering a tunnel. How do you do that?"

"It's easy," said Trev. "My brother showed me. You press two fingers on your tongue and…"

"NO!" the Angels shouted as one, covering their ears. Trev laughed, then started the engine of his car.

"Off to your brother's farm are you, Trev?" said Tarlock glumly. "Again."

Trev nodded. "Afraid so, Tarlock. I know having your coach missing isn't the best way to prepare for the new season, but my brother needs me more than the Angels at the moment. He's got flocks of sheep that need tending and he can't do that from his sickbed."

"Will he be better soon?" asked Daisy Higgins.

"He has to rest for a few more days," said Trev. "So in the meantime, Lennie will take charge of the training sessions – starting this morning, Lennie."

Lennie Gould, the Angels captain, stood up a little straighter. "OK, Trev. Anything in particular you want us to practise?"

Trev grinned. "Only one thing. The Angels code. One, two, three…"

"Angels on and off the pitch!" chanted the whole squad in unison.

"Brilliant," Trev shouted out of his car

window as he moved off. "Always remember that, and you won't go far wrong."

They watched him go. "Come on then," sighed Lennie. "Let's practise being Angels!"

⚽　　　⚽　　　⚽

They tried to act as if Trev really had been there with them. After some warm-up exercises, then spells of shooting and dribbling, they picked sides for a practice match.

Just as they were about to begin, though, they heard the fierce roar of a powerful

motorcycle and right up to the side of the pitch rode a huge man clad in leather. He pulled off his crash helmet.

"The name's Wally Sly," he called.

"What an ugly mug," hissed Rhoda O'Neill. "He looked better with his helmet on!"

Wally Sly looked them up and down. "So," he growled, "you're Saint Trev's goody-goodies, the famous Angels FC, are you? I'm told you lot all behave nearly as perfectly as he always did."

"Always did?" echoed Lennie. "You mean…you've seen Trev play?"

They'd all heard that Trev used to be a star player in his day.

"You could say that," snapped Sly. "It was awful. And I just can't believe he's coached a whole team to be like him – not a *successful* team, anyway."

Lennie gathered everybody together. "Right, let's show Slimy Sly how good a coach Trev is," he winked. "Bags of skill. And let's be *extra* angelic…"

They began their practice game. Almost

at once, Jonjo Rix won the ball and put his striking partner Colly Flower through. Racing to the edge of the penalty area, Colly hit a real whistler which was heading straight for the bottom corner of the goal – until Kirsten dived across and tipped it round the post!

"Ow!" Kirsten pretended to complain, sucking her fingers. "Hit it a bit softer next time, Colly!"

Colly immediately hurried up to her, looking as anxious as he could. "Oh, I'm truly sorry, Kirsten. Let me rub it better!"

From the touchline, Wally Sly roared with anger. "Rub it better? You should be threatening to break it next time!"

The game continued. Speedy Ricky King got the ball and set off at a blistering pace. Unable to keep up with him, Daisy Higgins pretended to grab Ricky's shirt – only to angelically let it go again.

"Sorry, Ricky!" she trilled sweetly. "You're too fast for me."

Ricky stopped dead. "No, no, I'm the one who's sorry, Daisy. Shall I wait for you to catch up?"

"What!" screamed Wally Sly. "You should be telling her she's as slow as a slug and scooting past her every chance you get!"

Then he turned his attention to Daisy. "And you should be pulling his shirt right off!" he hollered, fists clenched, "and his shorts as well if that's what it takes to stop him!"

"Trev wouldn't like that," said Daisy, shaking her head solemnly and trying not to laugh.

"Then he's as crummy a coach as I expected," scoffed Wally Sly.

And so it went on, with the Angels players apologising for every little thing, simply so that they could make Wally Sly jump up and down in a fury. And then, just before the end of the session, it all went wrong…

Lulu Squibb was put through on goal. Racing across, Bazza Watts mistimed his tackle and sent fiery Lulu flying. She was back on her feet at once, her eyes blazing.

"You big banana!" yelled Lulu, "do you know what I'm going to do to you?"

Wally Sly was overjoyed. "At last!" he yelled. "Go on, belt him! Flatten him! That's what you're going to do, isn't it?"

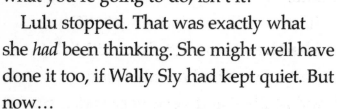

Lulu stopped. That was exactly what she *had* been thinking. She might well have done it too, if Wally Sly had kept quiet. But now…

"I'll tell you what I'm going to do to you, Bazza," she smiled through gritted teeth, "I'm going to give you a chance to say sorry for that tackle."

"Lulu, I'm sorry for that tackle," apologised Bazza at once, falling to his knees and polishing her boots with the sleeve of his shirt. "Forgive me!"

"Forgive you!" bawled Wally Sly. "I'd mangle every one of you! Call yourselves a football team? I could coach a team that would wipe the floor with you lot!"

The Angels had heard quite enough. "Why don't you, then?" cried Colly.

"We could do with an easy warm-up game before the season starts!" scoffed Rhoda.

"Then you'll see that Angels FC are coached by a winner!" shouted Mick Ryall.

Wally Sly smiled nastily…and thoughtfully…and very, very slyly. "So… supposing I did get a team together to play the Angels…you would expect the Angels coach to be the winning coach?"

They all walked straight into the trap.

As the rest of the Angels nodded enthusiastically in agreement Lennie yelled, "No doubt about it! The winning coach will be the Angels coach. And that's a promise!"

"Excellent!" said Wally Sly, triumphantly. "Then I *will* raise a team. And when they beat you, the winning coach will be the Angels coach. *Me!*"

"But – but –" stammered Lennie, realising what he'd been tricked into saying, "I didn't mean…"

"Of course you meant it, " said Sly, pulling on his helmet and revving up his motorcycle. "You promised!"

16

Trev returned just in time for the Sunday Club Night. All the Angels players were members of the St Jude's Youth Club, which Trev organised as vicar of St Jude's Church. They told him at once about Wally Sly's challenge – but, before they could mention any more, a motorcycle roared up outside. Seconds later, Wally Sly was barging his way through the door.

Trev smiled and held out a hand. "Mr Sly! Welcome! Good to see you again!"

The Angels exchanged glances. It was true. Trev and Wally Sly had met before. So were they friends? That question was answered immediately.

"The name's Wally," snarled Wally Sly. "Big Wally. And you can keep your welcome. Have they told you about the challenge match they promised to play?" Trev nodded. "Then just say you agree to it as well."

"Of course," said Trev. "If my team have made a promise, then that's it. Angels keep their promises. We'll be there."

"Excellent!" beamed Wally Sly. "So you'll be keeping the second part of the promise as well?"

Trev frowned. "The second part?"

Wally Sly glared at Lennie. "You haven't told him, have you? That's not very angelic, is it? Maybe you've forgotten what you did promise. Just as well I had this tucked under my leather jacket then, wasn't it?" And with that, Sly pulled out a portable tape recorder and pressed the button. Lennie's voice came out loud and clear: *No doubt about it! The winning coach will be the Angels coach. And that's a promise!*

Trev looked stunned. So stunned that, when Wally Sly said, "Agreed? The winning coach becomes the Angels coach!" and held out his hand, all Trev could do was shake it and seal Lennie's promise.

Lennie found the courage to speak up. "He won't win, Trev! We'll thump his team good and proper!"

Wally Sly guffawed. "Will you now? Well, I'll be coaching my team on the corner pitch in the park tomorrow evening. Come and watch us – if you're brave enough!"

"And, er…what is the name of your team?" asked Trev quietly.

"Villains United," growled Wally Sly. "And I do mean villains!"

2

The Villains Code

"S-sorry, Trev," stammered Lennie after Wally Sly had roared off on his motorcycle. The other Angels said the same.

Trev shook his head. "Don't worry. He tricked me too. We'll just have to show him that trickery doesn't pay. I've done it once before..."

The Angels coach disappeared before returning with a scrapbook. He flipped over the pages to reveal a yellowing newspaper cutting.

Sly-ding To Disaster!

The Amateur Cup Final at Wembley ended in complete humiliation for full-back Wally Sly yesterday. Given the run-around all afternoon by Trevor Rowe, who simply smiled and played on whenever he was fouled, Sly launched himself into a last-minute sliding tackle. But Rowe saw it coming. He stopped and, to the delight of the packed crowd, Sly slid on to demolish the advertising boards surrounding the pitch while Rowe raced away to score the winning goal...

"Wow! No wonder he doesn't like you," said Lennie. "You gave him the run-around and he's never forgotten it!"

"So how are we going to do the same this time, Trev?" said Colly, confident that their coach had a trick up his sleeve.

But Trev's face simply clouded over. "I don't know, Colly."

"He's not thinking straight," said Lulu as Trev drifted off. "He's worried about his brother – and now this."

"Then we'll have to help him," said Lennie. "We caused the trouble."

"So what are we going to do?" Daisy asked.

"Easy," said Lennie. "Spy on Sly!"

The corner pitch in the park was near a clump of trees and bushes. The next evening, behind every tree and bush there squatted an Angels player.

"Wally Sly hasn't made a very good start," hissed Lennie. "They haven't put up the goals on this pitch yet!"

"Bang goes shooting practice then," said Kirsten. "Unless Wally is going to have his strikers aiming for his mouth!"

"Too easy," laughed Jonjo. "They couldn't miss!"

Tarlock pointed across the park. In the distance the large figure of Wally Sly was heading their way, his team trooping behind.

Colly hooted. "Look! They haven't even got a football with them! What's he going to coach them in – conjuring goals out of thin air!"

It was a good joke, so Colly was surprised when nobody laughed. Then he saw why. Wally Sly's players had drawn near enough to be recognised – and the others had realised this challenge match was going to be deadly serious.

"He's got Hacker Haynes in his team," gasped Lennie. "The dirtiest player I've ever met!"[1]

"And Zippy Larkin," groaned Daisy. "Who chases racing cars for a hobby. He hates me."[2]

Mick Ryall goggled unhappily. "There's Bruiser Bloor! He'll be trying to bust my glasses again."[3]

[1] See *Dirty Defending!*
[2] See *Frightful Fouls!*
[3] See *Dazzling Dribbling!*

Behind his bush, Lionel was shaking like a leaf. "Look, even Nikki Sharpe's playing for them. She'll be after me for sure!"[4]

"That's why they haven't got a ball," groaned Ricky. "They'll be spending so much time kicking us they won't have time to kick the ball as well!"

Out on the pitch, Wally Sly had gathered his team together.

"Right, you Villains," shouted Sly, shaking his fists, "who wants to wallop Angels FC?"

[4] See *Suffering Substitutes!*

A forest of hands shot up. "We all do!" yelled Hacker Haynes. "We've all been made to look stupid by them. We want revenge!"

"And so do I," growled Sly fiercely. "I once had thousands of spectators laugh at me because of Saint Trev. Now I'm going to get my own back. I'm going to be the Angels coach and take his team away from him."

"But won't he just start up another team?" asked Nikki Sharpe.

"He can't, it's too late. The season's about to begin! We'll become Angels FC instead. Won't the other teams get a shock! While they're expecting us to be all goody-goody, we'll trample all over them and win everything!" Sly glared around at his players. "Just so long as you lot win this match."

"That's the problem, ennit?" scowled Bruiser Bloor. "None of us have ever played for a team that's beaten the Angels."

"Well you haven't had me coaching you before, have you?" snarled Sly. "Someone who can use your fouling talents to the full! Now, let's get started!"

Behind the trees and shrubs the Angels watched, horrified, as Wally Sly coached the Villains in how to shirt-pull, ankle-tap, body-check and foot-stamp without being spotted by the referee.

"So remember the Villains code," snarled Sly at the end of the session. "Villains all over the pitch!"

The Angels crept out from their hiding places shocked and shaking. Mick Ryall stammered, "Wh-what are we going to do?"

"Rely on Trev," said Lulu firmly. "I bet he'll come up with a tactic at tomorrow night's training session."

Lennie coughed. "Er… Trev won't be there. He's gone off to help his brother again. He's asked me to run it."

"But we need a tactic," yelled Lulu. "Otherwise the Villains will mangle us!"

"Got any suggestions?" asked Jonjo.

"Yes, I have," Lulu snarled. "Forget the Angels code. Let's practise Wally Sly's tactics – the Villains code!"

3

Ouch!

At the following night's training session they didn't bother with warming-up or shooting and dribbling exercises. Instead they went straight into a practice match.

"I don't want to hear anybody saying sorry!" yelled Lennie, shaking his fist.

"Anybody who says sorry to me," raged Lulu, "will be really sorry!"

They worked on shirt-pulling first. Bazza Watts and Mick Ryall were chosen to demonstrate. Mick dribbled mazily forward, but when he tried to race past

Bazza the full-back reached out, grabbed a handful of Mick's shirt, and yanked him backwards. Except that, not being used to playing dirty, Bazza yanked too hard. Instead of simply slowing Mick down, he dragged him backwards – with the result that Mick elbowed Bazza in the ribs and had his own ankle squashed by Bazza's boot!

"Ow!" groaned Bazza, clutching his side.

"Ooh!" moaned Mick, holding his ankle.

"You two had better take a rest," said Lennie. "But did everybody see how Bazza whacked Mick's ankle? Let's work on that!"

So they tried an ankle-tapping session.

Collecting the ball in midfield, Rhoda sprinted forward. Jeremy raced in at her from the right. Tarlock charged in from the left. Both were about to clout her on the ankles when Rhoda, realising that what was going to happen was going to hurt a lot, took fright – and stopped dead!

The result was chaos. Tarlock kicked Jeremy on the left ankle. Jeremy whacked Tarlock on the right shin. And, as they both hopped about in agony, they knocked Rhoda to the ground and crash-landed on her wrist!

"Ooh!" howled Jeremy.

"Eek!" gasped Tarlock.

"Agh!" screeched Rhoda.

Lennie groaned. "You three had better have a rest as well. Lulu and I will demonstrate making threats under our breath."

"Right," nodded Lulu. "I'll start."

She sidled up to Lennie and growled in his ear. "You big banana. Come near me and I'll give you a smack on the hooter."

Lennie snarled back, "You lumpy lemon. Touch me and I'll pull your ears off!"

Lulu turned and glared. "Pull my ears, you hairy horror, and I'll use your bonce as a football!"

"You pitiful prune," shouted Lennie, getting carried away, "do that and I'll tie a knot in your pigtails!"

"Oh yeah?" screeched Lulu, clenching her fists.

"Yeah!" bawled Lennie, his eyes popping.

Lulu poked Lennie in the chest. "Come on then, try it!"

Lennie twisted Lulu's nose. "Right, I will!"

And before anybody could stop them,

they began fighting in a blur of arms and legs. The scrap could have gone on for hours if it hadn't been ended by the fierce and totally unexpected shriek of a whistle.

"It's Trev!" cried Kirsten, "He's back! His brother must be better!"

The Angels coach was standing on the far side of the ground, his fingers still in his mouth. Meekly the squad limped and hobbled their way across to him.

"Is this what you call being Angels?" he said bleakly.

"Trev, let us explain…" began Lennie. After they'd told him about the Villains team and their nasty tactics, Trev looked even more serious.

"Have you got a crafty tactic yet, Trev?" asked Ricky anxiously.

"No, I'm afraid I haven't."

"But you've got to think of something!" wailed Lionel. "If we lose this game you won't be the Angels coach any more and we won't be the Angels and...and..." His voice cracked and he buried his face in his shirt.

"Think, Trev. *Please*," urged Tarlock. "You've given Wally Sly the run-around before. You can do it again."

Trev suddenly brightened. "The run-around, eh?" he murmured. "Now there's a thought..." He turned on his heel and strode off.

"Where are you going?" called Jeremy.

"To invite Wally Sly to a meeting in the Club Room tomorrow evening. See you all there!"

4

Bob Who?

The Club Room looked like a hospital's
Accident and Emergency department.
Mick and Jeremy had bandaged ankles.
Tarlock had a lump on his shin. Rhoda
was nursing her bandaged wrist and,
under his shirt, Bazza was hiding his
bandaged ribs. As for Lennie and Lulu,
they were covered in so many bruises
they'd lost count.

The door opened. Into the room stepped
a solemn-looking Trev followed by a
beaming Wally Sly.

"Oh dear," Sly chuckled nastily when he saw the wounded Angels. "What have you lot done to yourselves? You're not going to give my Villains much of a match, are you? Still, never mind. I won't be needing most of you when I take over as the Angels coach. I don't have weaklings in my teams."

"You won't be taking over, Mr Sly," said Trev quietly. "I will still be the Angels coach after this game because my Angels are going to beat your Villains."

Wally Sly snorted. "No chance! Saturday is going to be your unlucky day!"

"Luck will have nothing to do with it," said Trev, coolly. He paused, then added gently, "but if it does, then we'll have our lucky mascot to help us out."

"I didn't know we had a mascot," said Kirsten.

"Saturday will be his first appearance," said Trev. "His name's Bob. He lives with my brother on his farm." He glanced at Wally Sly. "I was wondering…perhaps we could have a special rule, just for this game. That mascots could play for their teams in the second half."

Wally Sly looked suspicious. "How old is this Bob? How big is he? How good is he?" Trev answered the three questions without hesitation. "Bob's four years old, he's about knee-high…and he's never played football in his life before."

"And you want to bring him on? You must be desperate!"

"You agree then?" said Trev.

Wally Sly looked thoughtful. "So long as the Villains can bring on their lucky mascot as well."

Trev shook his hand. "Agreed. What's your mascot's name?"

"Wally," chuckled the Villains coach gleefully. "Wally Sly. It's me!"

"But that's not fair!" cried the whole Angels squad.

"But nothing! It's was your coach's idea, not mine. He could have made himself your mascot, but he wasn't bright enough to think of that. So now you're stuck with little Bob." Wally guffawed loudly as he left. "See you on Saturday, then – with my biggest boots on!"

The Angels looked miserably at each other. Half of them were injured and in three day's time they were going to be up against the meanest team that had ever been formed. As if that wasn't bad enough, Trev had just allowed himself to be tricked into allowing Wally Sly to come on for the Villains as well!

"I hope Bob is a four-year-old genius, Trev," said Bazza Watts. "When are we going to meet him?"

"Saturday," said Trev. "I'll bring him back with me that morning."

All around the room faces fell. "You mean," said Lennie, "you're going off again?"

Trev nodded. "I'm afraid so. My brother's

much better, but it's a really busy time on the farm. The sheep all have to be brought in from the fields, and I'm not as experienced at it as he is. I'm improving, though…"

But the Angels weren't listening. Trev's great tactic had turned out to be a complete dud and they were going to get mangled by the Villains.

For the first time ever, none of them were looking forward to playing their next match.

5

Angels v Villains

"Where's your coach, then?" sneered Wally
Sly as the Angels dawdled out on to the
pitch on Saturday morning. "Too frightened
to come and watch the slaughter, is he?"

The Angels all looked desolate.
They'd been miserable before, but
nothing compared to how they felt now.
Trev hadn't arrived.

"He'll be here," retorted Lennie bravely.
"He must have been held up in the traffic."

"With little Bobby-wobby?" smirked
Wally Sly. "Ah, what a pity. Still we can't

wait for him. The game must go on." The Villains coach ruffled Lennie's hair with his huge paw. "Come on, look on the bright side, it will all be over in an hour or so."

He's right, thought Lennie gloomily. That's just what it will be for the Angels – all over.

The Villains had learned their lessons well. The moment the match began, they were at their meanest and sneakiest.

With only five minutes gone, speedy Zippy Larkin chased after a through ball for the Villains. But Daisy Higgins had seen it coming. Turning in good time, she was just about to kick the ball safely into touch when...

"How does this grab you, Daisy?" called
Zippy Larkin – and pulled her back by the
shirt! Put out of her stride, Daisy could do
nothing to stop him overtaking her and
whacking the ball into the Angels net to put
Villains 1–0 ahead!

Ten minutes later, disaster struck again.
Mick Ryall got the ball in a crowded
midfield. In jumped Bruiser Bloor – and

down went Mick, glasses flying and clutching his already injured ankle. Worse, as the ball ran free, Bloor played it through for Zippy Larkin to score again.

Angels 0, Villains 2!

"Didn't see that one coming, did you four-eyes?" laughed Bruiser Bloor as Mick limped off, to be replaced by substitute Ricky King.

The Angels went on the attack. Then in another crowded midfield tussle, Hacker Haynes elbowed Bazza in the ribs while the referee wasn't looking, then whacked the ball upfield for Zippy Larkin to outrun Jeremy Emery and score yet again!

Villains 3, Angels 0 – and, with Bazza also being too hurt to continue, on trotted a very anxious Lionel Murgatroyd to replace him.

"We've just got to try to hang on until half-time without letting in another goal," Lulu told him. "Maybe Trev will be here by then."

"Bang on till tough-time," stammered Lionel, tongue-tied with nerves. "KO."

Seeing this, Villains' Nikki Sharpe lost no time in whispering menacingly into Lionel's ear, "Coo-ee! Lionel! I'm going to kick yooouuu! Very *haa-rrdd!*"

The threat worked. When the ball came Lionel's way, he was quivering with fear so much that he didn't even notice he was facing his own goal. Desperately lashing out at the ball before Nikki Sharpe could get to him, Lionel could only look on horrified as it zoomed into the air, did a loop or two, then rocketed down past Kirsten and into the Angels net!

4–0 to Villains United at half-time!

"Where's Trev?" moaned Colly as the shell-shocked Angels slumped on the ground. "We need him!"

"Here he comes!" whooped Lulu.

Screeching his car to a halt, Trev ran to the back, lifted the tailgate – and out hopped a black and white sheepdog.

"What's this?" growled Wally Sly when Trev raced over with the dog trotting beside him.

"Our mascot," smiled Trev. "Bob. Four years old and no higher than your knee. And, as we agreed, I'd like him to play for the Angels in the second half."

"No chance," said Wally Sly. "Dogs are not allowed."

Trev sighed. "I see. Well, if you're going back on your promise, Mr Sly, I don't see why my players shouldn't go back on theirs…"

That made the Villains coach change his mind very quickly. "All right, Bob can play for you! But…" Sly added slyly, "if he bares his teeth, then it counts as dangerous play, which is a yellow card offence. Right, Ref?"

The referee nodded in agreement, continuing to nod as Wally Sly went on, "Barking or snarling counts as ungentlemanly conduct and both get yellow cards as well. Two offences and Bob's sent off. And if he bites anyone he's really in the dog house – he gets sent off straight away!"

"I agree," said Trev.

"And if he touches the ball with anything but his nose, then it's the same as a handball," said Wally Sly.

"That's fine too," said Trev. "Bob won't be touching the ball."

The Angels' mouths dropped open in surprise. "Won't be touching the ball?" gasped Bazza. "Then what's he going to do?"

"He's going to listen to my whistling," laughed Trev. "Now come on, Angels. Get out there and play your normal game!"

Still mystified, the Angels lined up for the start of the second half. And they grew even more mystified when Bob didn't join them, but simply laid down on the touchline close by Trev's feet.

But the moment the game restarted and Villains surged forward with Zippy Larkin on the ball, Trev gave a loud, long, low whistle. Off shot Bob, racing across the pitch! Without touching the ball, Bob raced back and forth in front of the Villains player. Zippy Larkin found his way barred and had to screech to a halt.

"Foul, Ref!" bawled Wally Sly.

"Nonsense!" called the referee, "he's simply jockeying your player. All defenders do it. Perfectly legal!"

Trev whistled again. A short, sharp one this time. Bob instantly changed direction and began to steer Zippy Larkin back towards the centre circle. Hacker Haynes raced forward, calling for a pass. Trev whistled again – and Bob immediately switched his attention to race in front of Haynes as if he was herding sheep and Haynes was a runaway!

"Look!" cried Colly Flower. "Bob's bunching the Villains together as if they were a flock! They can't get near us to do their dirty tricks!"

Completely put off by Bob's antics, Zippy Larkin lost control of the ball. Tarlock nipped in and played it forward. Rhoda took it on. By the time she laid it into Jonjo's path on the edge of the Villains penalty area, Bob had raced forward and was rounding up their defenders into a little group. All Jonjo had to do was run forward and smash the ball into the Villains net!

Within a few minutes, Angels had scored again. Colly scorched through on a run. Bruiser Bloor charged at him, ready to pull his shirt and tap his ankle for good measure. Trev whistled again. Instantly a black and white blur shot in front of Bloor to steer him away from Colly – who, able to use his skill, ran on and planted the ball into the Villains net. Angels 2, Villains 4!

"Bob's giving them the run-around," shouted Tarlock. "Just like Trev did to Wally Sly that time!"

"And Sly knows it!" yelled Jeremy. "Look, he's running away!"

It certainly seemed so. Furiously, the Villains coach had jammed his crash helmet on his head, skidded out of the ground and was roaring off down the road.

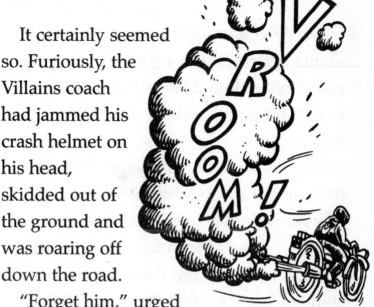

"Forget him," urged Tarlock, "we've got a game to win!"

It was all one-way traffic now. With Bob obeying Trev's every whistled command to herd Villains out of harm's way, the Angels could play without fear of being fouled. A quick one-two between Lulu and Rhoda sent Lulu racing through to hammer in another goal for the Angels.

"Angels 3, Big Bananas 4!" screamed Lulu. "Let's score another one!"

The Angels mounted attack after attack. Rhoda scraped the bar with a rocket shot and Lennie came close with a looping header from one of Ricky King's long throws.

Then Lionel Murgatroyd got the ball on the halfway line. He dribbled forward, looking anxiously to one side as Nikki Sharpe charged in to tackle him – only to see her veer off in the opposite direction as Bob bounded up to protect him. Lionel dribbled on. Other Villains came towards him but couldn't get close to the ball as Bob circled round Lionel like a four-legged force field.

Lionel suddenly realised he was close to the Villains goal. But how could he shoot with Bob dashing in front of him all the time? He needn't have worried. Trev had the situation under control. Two short, sharp whistles – and Bob instantly sat down at Lionel's side. All Lionel had to do was hammer the ball left-footed into the Villains' goal.

4–4 and still five minutes to go!

The Angels raced back to the centre circle. They were joined by Bob who immediately lay down on the halfway line, his ears pricked as he listened for Trev's next command. What he and everybody else heard instead, though, was the shattering roar of a motorcycle.

"It's Wally!" cheered the Villains. "He's back!"

Careering into the ground, Wally Sly skidded to a halt at the very edge of the pitch. "Ref!" he bellowed, "I'm coming on as my team's lucky mascot!"

Striding on to the pitch, the Villains coach called his team together and muttered some instructions before the Villains kicked off.

When they did, Zippy Larkin, as instructed, passed the ball to Wally Sly – who promptly planted one heavy foot it, making it impossible for an Angels player to kick away.

Then he dug something out of his pocket and tossed it towards Bob. The sheepdog's nose twitched. He licked his lips. And then he began to gnaw.

"What have you given him?" cried Lulu.

"A tasty, roast bone," laughed Wally Sly. "I've just been to a pet shop to get it. Now you'll see some crafty coaching. Surround that dog, Villains!"

Before the Angels could move, the whole Villains team had raced forward, dropping to their knees to encircle the crunching Bob.

"Now keep him there," growled Sly, "until I put this on him!" Out of his pocket he pulled something else he'd bought from the pet shop – an ugly-looking collar and lead. Murmuring, "Good boy. Stay…" Wally Sly crept towards Bob. Closer and closer until, with Sly no more than a metre away, the air was split by the loudest, longest, shrillest, whistle Trev had ever produced.

Instantly Bob left his tasty bone, leaping high out from the circle of Villains as they tried to grab him. Desperately, Wally Sly dived headlong to try and stop Bob escaping – only to land on top of his own players!

"Aggh!" they all screamed as Wally Sly squashed them into the mud.

"The ball!" yelled Kirsten from her goal. "He's left the ball!"

She was right. In creeping forward to try to collar Bob, Wally Sly had taken his foot off the ball. It was free.

"Captain's ball!" screamed Lennie Gould joyfully.

And, leaving behind the whole Villains team as they struggled to free themselves from beneath the vast shape of Wally Sly, Lennie simply had to dribble the ball the length of the field and tap it into the empty Villains net.

Immediately there came another, very different, whistle – the referee's, blowing for full-time. Angels had won 5–4! The whole team raced to surround Trev and the tail-wagging Bob.

"Three cheers for Trev the Rev, our crafty coach!" shouted Lennie.

"For ever and ever, amen!" yelled the others.

Trev smiled broadly. "Angels, you make coaching a pleasure. And that's something not all coaches are able to say. Ask Wally Sly!"

Out in the centre-circle, the Villains had freed themselves and were now angrily jumping up and down on their moaning, groaning coach.

"He doesn't seem to be enjoying his job, Trev," laughed Lennie.

"That's what happens when you're in charge of a team who don't play by the rules, Lennie," said Trev. "Coaching becomes a dog's life!"

⚽ ANGELS F.C. ⚽

MICHAEL COLEMAN
ILLUSTRATED BY NICK ABADZIS

Collect all these sharpshooting soccer stories!